MARTIN THE COBBLER

Adapted from a story by LEO TOLSTOY.

Illustrated with stills of the animated, clay figures
from the award-winning film by Billy Budd, Inc.

Copyright © 1982 by Billy Budd Films, Inc.
All rights reserved. No part of this book may be
reproduced or used in any form except for promotional
purposes without written permission from the
copyright holder.
Library of Congress Catalog Card Number: 82-70486
ISBN: 0-86683-638-1
Printed in the United States of America.
5 4 3 2 1

Book design: Nancy Condon

Winston Press, Inc.
430 Oak Grove
Minneapolis, Minnesota 55403

In a certain town there lived a cobbler, Martin Avdéich by name. He was a good cobbler, honest and fair with his prices. And many people brought their boots to him to be fixed. There was hardly a pair of boots in the village that he did not know by sight.

But Martin was unhappy. It seemed to him that there was nothing left to live for. Oh, there was his work . . . but the work was becoming harder and harder. His hands had become unsteady through the years, and his eyes had dimmed from the hours of close work.

When he was a young man, he had a family to live for. But alas, tragedy struck fast and Martin lost his oldest child and his wife, leaving him with a baby boy to care for. He had always been a good man and cared well for the child. But as fate would have it, just when the boy reached an age when he could help his father, he fell ill and died.

Martin gave way to despair, and in his sorrow he blamed the Lord for taking his family away from him. He wished that he would die, too.

For Martin, the days passed almost unnoticed, one after the other. Martin paid attention only to his work.

Then one day an old pilgrim visited Martin. "Holy man, why have you come to see me?" asked Martin.

"I was told I would find an expert cobbler on the other side of this door."

"That you have, pilgrim," replied Martin. "Come in. What is it that you had in mind? New soles? New heels?"

"No, Martin. What I need is a new binding for this ancient book of the Lord," answered the pilgrim. "This holy book has been handed down from pilgrim to pilgrim, and I bring it to you so that it may be preserved and protected for ages to come."

"I am greatly honored," Martin began, "but I am afraid you have come to the wrong cobbler. God and I have not been getting on well. Take this precious book to someone more holy than I."

"Tell me," asked the pilgrim, "what is this trouble between you and the Lord?"

"I am without hope, holy man." Martin explained sadly all that had happened to him over the years. "All I ask of God is that I may soon die."

"Perhaps you are in despair, Martin, because you live only for yourself," said the pilgrim.

Martin looked up questioningly. "What else is there to live for?"

"For God, Martin. He gives you life . . . and you must live for him. Here, read the book if you like. Perhaps it will help."

"I must leave now," said the pilgrim, "for a long journey lies ahead of me. Take care, Martin. I will return for the book. Farewell."

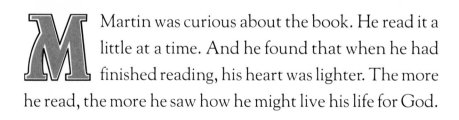

Martin was curious about the book. He read it a little at a time. And he found that when he had finished reading, his heart was lighter. The more he read, the more he saw how he might live his life for God.

One part of the book told how a rich merchant invited the Lord to be his guest but did not treat Him as a guest, did not welcome Him. Martin thought to himself, "Why, that rich merchant must be like me. He, too, thought only of himself. No care for his guest. Yet it was the Lord who was his guest. If He came to me would I act like that?" Martin shook his head. "No, if the Lord were my guest I would give Him all the signs of welcome." Then Martin, becoming drowsy, laid his head on his arms and fell asleep.

"Martin!" He suddenly heard a voice, as if someone had breathed the word above his ear.

He started from his sleep. "Who's there?" he asked.

He turned around and looked at the door; no one was there. Then he heard, "Martin, Martin! Look out into the street tomorrow, for I shall come." Martin did not know whether he was dreaming or had really heard the words. He decided it was time for bed.

N Next morning he rose before daylight, lit the fire, and prepared his breakfast. Then he sat down at his bench by the window. As he worked, Martin thought over what had happened the night before. At times it seemed like a dream, and at times he thought he had really heard the voice.

So he sat by the window, and whenever anyone passed by in unfamiliar boots, he would stop and look up to see not only the feet of the passerby but the face as well.

Presently, an old soldier named Stepanich came near the window to clear away the snow with his shovel. Martin knew him by his felt boots which were old and shabby, with leather bottoms. Martin glanced at Stepanich and went on with his work.

"I must be growing crazy with age," said Martin to himself. "Stepanich comes to clear away the snow, and I imagine it's the Lord coming to visit me. Foolish old man that I am."

Martin made a few more stitches and then felt drawn to the window again. Old Stepanich looked tired and weak. He was trying to warm himself.

"What if I called him in and gave him some tea?" thought Martin. He made some tea and then tapped the window with his fingers. Stepanich turned and came to the window. Martin beckoned him in and went himself to open the door.

"Come in," said Martin. "Come and warm yourself a bit. I'm sure you must be cold."

"God bless you!" Stepanich answered. "My bones do ache, to be sure."

"Ah, such tea," sighed Stepanich when he'd finished his. "It's very good."

"Here," said Martin, "let me pour you another cup."

Stepanich noticed that Martin kept looking out toward the street. "Are you expecting someone?" he asked.

Martin smiled. "Am I expecting someone? Well now, I'm ashamed to tell you. It isn't that I really expect someone, but I heard something last night that made me think the Lord is going to visit me today. I can't get the idea out of my mind, and I keep looking for him."

Stepanich nodded his head and finished his tea, saying, "Thank you, Martin. You have given me food for body and soul."

"You're very welcome. Come again another time. I am glad to have a guest," said Martin.

Stepanich went away, and Martin poured out the last of the tea and drank it up. Then he put away the tea things and sat down to his work, stitching the back seam of a boot. And as he stitched he kept looking out of the window, thinking about the Lord's promise to visit him.

Two soldiers went by: one in government boots, the other in boots Martin had made; then the master of a neighboring house, in shining galoshes; then a baker carrying a basket. Then a woman passed the window, but stopped by the wall. Martin glanced up at her and saw that she was a stranger, poorly dressed and with a baby in her arms. She had her back to the wind, trying to protect the baby with the little wrapping she used as a blanket. Through the window Martin heard the baby crying and the woman trying to soothe it. Martin hurried to the door and called to her.

"My dear! I say, my dear!"

The startled woman turned around.

"Why do you stand out there with the baby in the cold? Come inside. You can wrap him up better in a warm place. Come this way."

The woman was surprised to see an old man in an apron calling to her, but she followed him in.

"There, my dear. Sit down near the stove," invited Martin. "Warm yourself and eat some porridge while I mind the baby. I have had children of my own."

After the woman finished her porridge, she began to tell Martin her story.

"I'm a soldier's wife," she said. "They sent my husband somewhere far away eight months ago, and I have heard nothing of him since. I had a place as cook, but after my baby was born they would not allow me to stay. For three months now I have been struggling, unable to find a place, and I've had to sell all I had for food."

Martin sighed, "Haven't you any warmer clothing?" he asked.

"No," the woman replied sadly. "I had to pawn my shawl just this morning."

Martin gently handed the child back to the woman and went to look through some clothes hanging on the wall. He brought out an old cloak.

"Here," he said, "though it's old and worn out, it will keep you both warm."

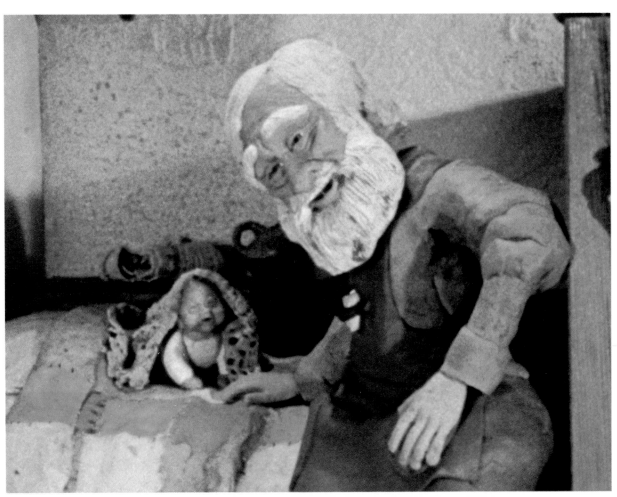

The woman looked at the cloak, then at the old man, and taking it, burst into tears.

"Bless you, my friend," she sobbed. "Surely the Lord must have sent me to your window."

Martin smiled. "Yes, it was no mere chance that made me look out today." And he told the woman his dream and how he had heard the Lord's voice promising to visit him that day.

"Who knows? All things are possible," said the woman, wrapping the cloak round herself and the baby. Then she bowed and thanked Martin once more.

After the woman had gone, Martin ate some cabbage soup, cleared the things away, and sat down to work again. But he did not forget the window, and every time a shadow fell on it, he looked up at once to see who was passing.

After a while Martin saw an apple-woman stop in front of his window. She had a large basket, which she had set down a moment while she rested. Just then a boy in a tattered cap ran up, snatched an apple from the basket, and tried to slip away. But the woman saw him and caught the boy by his sleeve. The boy began to struggle, but the old woman knocked his cap off and seized hold of his hair. Martin dropped his work and ran out into the street.

"Why you little rascal!" the old woman was scolding. "You know better than to steal. I'm going to teach you a lesson."

Martin separated the two, taking the boy by the hand. "Let him go, Granny. Let him go."

"I'll make him pay," the old woman protested. "I'll take him to the police."

"He won't do it again," Martin pleaded. "Let the boy go."

The old woman let go, and the boy began to cry and say he was sorry.

"That's right," Martin said to the boy, "and don't do it again. Now here's an apple for you." Then to the old woman, "I will pay you, Granny."

"You will spoil the rascal that way," said the old woman. "He should be whipped so that he will remember it for a week."

"Oh, Granny, Granny," said Martin, "that's our way—but it's not God's way. If he should be whipped for an apple, what should be done to us?"

The old woman was silent.

"God bids us forgive," said Martin. "Forgive everyone, and a thoughtless youngster most of all."

The old woman wagged her head and sighed.

"It's true enough," said she, "but they are getting terribly spoilt."

"Then we old ones must show them better ways," Martin replied.

The boy was listening quietly now, and as the old woman was about to lift up her basket, the lad sprang forward. "Let me carry it for you, Granny," he offered. "I'm going that way."

The old woman nodded her head, and they went down the street together, chatting as they walked.

When they were out of sight, Martin went back to the house. He finished off one boot and, turning it about, examined it. It was all right. He gathered his tools together, swept up the cuttings, and put away the bristles and the thread and the awls. Then he placed the lamp on the table. He took the holy book from the shelf. He meant to open it at the place he had marked the day before, but the book opened at another place. As he opened it, Martin's dream came back to him, and no sooner had he thought of it then he seemed to hear footsteps, as though someone were moving behind him. Martin turned around, and it seemed to him as if people were standing in the dark corner, but he could not make out who they were. A voice whispered in his ear:

"Martin, Martin, don't you know me?"

"Who is it?" murmured Martin.

"It is I," said the voice. And out of the dark corner stepped Stepanich, who smiled and, vanishing like a cloud, was seen no more.

"It is I," said the voice again. And out of the darkness stepped the woman with the baby in her arms, and the woman smiled and the baby laughed, and they too vanished.

"It is I," said the voice once more. And the old woman and the boy with the apple stepped out and both smiled, and then they too vanished.

Martin's soul grew glad. He began reading the book just where it had opened, and at the top of the page he read:

"I was hungry, and you gave me food; I was thirsty, and you gave me drink; I was a stranger, and you took me in."

And at the botton of the page he read:

"Inasmuch as you did it unto one of these you did it unto me."

Then Martin understood that his dream had come true and that the Lord had really come to him that day, and Martin had welcomed him.